Legends of the

Blue Willow Story

Jennifer C. Petersen

Printed in the United States of America.

First Printing, 2020

Tea Trade Mart Publishing

800 NE Tenney Rd 110-429

Vancouver, WA 98685

www.jenniferpetersen.com

ISBN: 978-0-9984102-7-2

PREFACE

What could be better than crafting our own love stories based upon a blue and white dish? Blue Willow tea ware, china cabinets filled with Blue Willow, poetry, theatrical plays, children's play sets, fabrics and accessories, games and more – derived from inspiration by Chinese art and customs. What a legacy!

Nearly 250 years have passed since the design and manufacture of one of the world's most popular and humble china pattern – Legends of Blue Willow. Envisioned as a marketing message, the Blue Willow story blossomed beyond what the manufacturers ever imagined.

This book briefly introduces you to the potter, designer and background of the commercial aspect of Blue Willow.

From the busy world of pottery, we are captivated by legends that arose from speculation centered around a willow tree, a powerful mandarin, his exceptionally beautiful daughter, an elderly but wealthy duke and the mandarin's daughter's heart choice, a brilliant but lowly accounting secretary.

Let your imagine flow with the legends then perhaps you'll write your own Blue Willow legend.

TABLE OF CONTENTS

INTRODUCTION

Two pigeons flying high,
Chinese vessel sailing by,
Weeping willow hanging o'er,
Bridge with three men – if not four.
Chinese Temple, there it stands,
Seems to cover all the land;
Apple tree with apples on,
A pretty fence to end my song.

A Fine Old Spode Soup Tureen Stand
Showing the "Dagger" Border

China, the name applied to the best kinds of pottery and porcelain indicates its origin; and the name China is applied with equal intelligibility to the ornaments on the mantelpiece, the crockery in the closet, and to that vast empire which stretches from the north to the south of the east coast of Asia.

We are indebted to China for many articles in daily use; and it is certain that the Chinese were acquainted with the use of spectacles and magnifying glasses, gunpowder, and cast iron, long before the light of civilization had reached our shores.

The term "Willow" is applied in a general way to many of the copies of the blue and white Oriental porcelain imported from China during the last half of the 18th century. However, the willow pattern is of the same design as a Chinese plate, which Caughley[i] copied. Adaptations vary widely.

Whether the story was invented by some ingenious person to fit the plate, no one knows; but it is a strong possibility.

On Chinese plates, the *dramatis personae* are missing. The willow has always been a sorrowful tree, where historically those who have lost their loves make their mourning garlands. "I offered him my company to a willow tree .... to make him a Garland as being forsaken," says Benedick in *Much Ado About Nothing*.

The poem in the opening paragraph and the following paragraphs are brief love stories that are told concerning the willow plate.

Chang, the secretary of a Mandarin whose house is on the right side of the plate, dared to love his master's daughter, Li-Chi. But the Mandarin had other plans and his daughter was promised to an old but wealthy suitor.

To prevent the lovers from meeting, the Mandarin imprisoned his daughter in a room in his house overlooking the water.

A correspondence ensued, so the story goes, between the lovers and the lady sent a poetical message in a coconut shell, floating down the river, that she expected Chang when the willow leaf commenced to fall.

By the connivance of a gardener, who apparently lived in the small cottage on the left, overshadowed by a fir tree, the lovers escaped, and are depicted as fleeing over the bridge – the Mandarin behind with a whip in his hand, the lady in front, and Chang in the middle carrying a jewel box.

The individual in the junk, higher up, is intended to denote that they fled to the island in the northwest of the plate.

They lived happily until Fate, in the shape of the wealthy lover, overtook them and burned their house to ashes. However, the gods changed them into two doves, which, of course, figure prominently in the design.

This tragic story of disastrous love has clung to the willow pattern plates, and nobody can shake the belief of the owners of different specimens of the middle 19th century days that these plates are of great value.

The original design was shades of blue. Blue is the chief underglaze color to be considered in connection with underglaze transfer printing. There was a great demand for deep blues and for lighter blue, both of which came from the Staffordshire earthenware printers and potters from English porcelain factories such as Caughley, where sometime around 1780, Thomas Turner, an apprentice at Worcester under Robert Hancock (the pioneer engraver of copper plates by transfer printing), made his famous "willow pattern"; conversely the idea may have derived straight from the Chinese blue porcelain underglaze of Nankin, so much in vogue in middle eighteenth century era.

"Nanking" porcelain, often confused with Blue Willow ware, was export ware decorated in blue on white, made at Ching-te-chen and shipped from the port of Nanking; polychromed export porcelain was shipped through Canton.

John Turner of Lane End (not to be confused with Thomas Turner of Caughley) was the first to print underglaze blue in Staffordshire. Josiah Spode, about 1784, introduced his underglaze blue "willow pattern" a copy of the Caughley pattern .

William Adams of Greengates, in 1787, brought out his underglaze blue, which some say has never been surpassed for richness and mellowness.

In 1787, Thomas Minton, now a master potter at Stoke, formerly an apprentice at Caughley with Thomas Turner, designed the celebrated "Broseley Dragon" pattern tea service for porcelain in 1782 (following the willow pattern, 1780) and produced in the late years of the eighteenth century about 1793, some fine blue-printed ware at Stoke.

Our present manufacturers have far outshone, and surpassed, the beauty of material and the pottery of the old Chinese specimens, but fashion still gives preference to Chinese patterns and forms.

A remarkable instance of this preference is to be found in the fact that the sale of the common blue plate, known as "willow pattern", exceeds that of all others put together. The name is derived from the figure of the tree which occupies the center of the plate, and which is intended to represent a willow in spring, which unfolds its blossoms before its leaves appear.

Quoting from a lecture given by Reverend Henry Allen, who says: "The most remarkable development of the potter's art pertains to those queer, incarnate types of antiquity, the Chinese. While the art of tempering and glazing was disappearing in Europe, the Chinese and their neighbors, the Japanese, had been for centuries making that peculiar porcelain with which, in its grotesque determination to put down all tyrannical laws of perspective and proportion, you are all familiar.

Who is there who has not photographed upon his brain every line and dot of the immortal blue willow pattern? A pattern named on account of its astounding willow, with its four bunches of triple prince's feathers for foliage, and its inconceivable root growing out of an impossible soil; its magical bridge suspended like a leaping squirrel between earth and heaven; its three Chinese mermen (a fabled marine creature with the head and upper body of a man and the tail of a fish), working themselves upon their tails, in some inscrutable way or other, into the funny little temple in the corner; the allegorical ship that sales in midair over the tops of it, through which it threatens to thrust its mast; the two nondescript birds, which would defy even the anatomy of Owen (a Herculean figure), billing and cooing in their uncouth Chinese fashion beside the strange blue tree with round plum-pudding leaves, a permanent puzzle to botanists, and which grows out of the top of another temple with three deep blue columns, and beneath which a mysterious stream flows – which sublime landscape, for millions of ages and upon tens of millions of plates has represented to the world the artistic ideas of the Raphaels of the cerulean empire."

Who is there, since the earliest dawn of intelligent perception, who has not inquisitively contemplated the mysterious figures on the willow pattern plate?

Who, in childish curiosity, has not wondered what those three persons in the dim blue outline did upon that bridge - where they came from, and where they were going! Why is the boatman without oars on that wide stream?

Who lived in the houses on that charmed island? And why do those disproportionate doves forever kiss each other, as if intensely joyful over some good deed done?

Who of us has not wondered about such things as we found our eyes resting upon the willow pattern plates as they graced the dinner table or brightly gleamed on the cottage plate rail?

The old willow pattern plate! By every association, in spite of its lack of artistic beauty, it is dear to us. It is mingled with our earliest recollections; it is like the picture of an old friend and companion whose portrait we see everywhere, but of whose likeness we never grow weary.

Its charms are unchanged, whether we view it as a flat oval dish – rounded into a cheese plate – hollowed out into a soup tureen or contorted into the shape of a ladle! Still, in every change of form there are three blue people rushing over the bridge; still the boatman sits listless on the stream, and the doves are constantly kissing and fluttering in great glorification at the result.

What it is all about? Let's explore the willow plate pattern and imagine the scenes through the following stories, which are said to be to the Chinese what our "Jack the Giant Killer", or "Robinson Crusoe", is to us.

Herein are some, but not all, legends of the willow pattern plate.

Thomas Turner, Potter

Caughley ware, porcelain produced by the Caughley China Works, was a British pottery factory in Caughley, Shropshire, England, established about 1751, for making earthenware. It was managed by Mr. Brown, of Caughley Hall, and after his death by Mr. Gallimore. It was not until 1772, when porcelain was first made, that it rose to any importance when Thomas Turner, Mr. Gallimore's successor, commenced operations. He came from the Worchester porcelain manufacture which he left on the sale of the works.

Thomas Turner (1749 – February 1809) was an English potter. It is believed that Turner was brought up as a silversmith. He was formally apprenticed to his father which qualified him for the esteemed designation "freedom of the city of Worcester". In addition to being made a free man of the city of Worchester and two other boroughs, he was a justice of the peace for Shropshire. These fortunate circumstances helped direct his efforts and secured his success.

It is probable that he was connected with the Worcester china works in his early years. He was an excellent chemist, a master of the various processes connected with porcelain manufacture, a skillful draftsman, designer, and engraver. He was a magistrate for Shropshire and Staffordshire, and a freeman of Worcester, Much Wenlock, and Bridgnorth.

The Caughley or Salopian Porcelain Factory was established by Turner in the early 1770s, possibly on the site of a pre-existing pottery factory and perhaps initially in partnership with Ambrose Gallimore.

In the mid-1760's, Thomas Turner came from Worcester where as an apprentice (probably under Robert Hancock) he learned the art of engraving on copper plates and transferring the designs to porcelain. These techniques were fully exploited at Caughley where 80% of the wares were decorated in underglaze blue usually from copper plates.

In 1772, Turner succeeded Gallimore (brother-in-law of Josiah Spode) as lessee of the porcelain factory at Caughley in Shropshire. Gallimore had obtained the lease to the works, styled 'The Salopian China Warehouse' in 1754. Under Turner's management, their reputation grew rapidly.

One distinction of the factory was its introduction of the perennial Willow pattern; the original, dated 1779, was intended for a teapot, and the best-known version was developed by Turner in the late 1780s. Blue Willow ware was produced by many subsequent factories, perhaps the most widespread of domestic designs.

Thomas Turner made the first full table service of printed ware in England. His ware was of excellent quality, but limited to useful articles, and unfortunately not all his specimens are marked. Early pieces printed in underglaze blue resemble the early Worchester blue and white, but Caughley is whiter in appearance and the blue is not as mellow as that of Worchester. The Caughley blue is usually

Willow pattern on a creamware teapot attributed to John Warburton, Staffordshire, England, c. 1800; in the Victoria and Albert Museum, London.

characterized by the brightness of the blue and intensity of tint somewhat exaggerated. The colors were of such secrecy that Turner mixed all the ingredients himself.

The Caughley Porcelain Factory was operating commercially by 1775 when the first commercial advertisements appeared. Products included tea sets, muffin plates, butter tubs, mugs, mask jugs, egg cups and drainers, custard cups, pickle shells, eye baths, asparagus servers and toy tea and table wares.

"The porcelain factory erected near Bridgenorth in this county is now quite complete, and the proprietors have received and supplied orders to a very large amount. Lately, we saw some of their productions, which in color and fineness are truly elegant and beautiful, and have the bright and lively white of the so much extolled Oriental", newspaper article dated November 1, 1775.

"In the early years of the Caughley manufactory, the ware was considered only slightly better than earthenware; but it gradually assumed a finer and more transparent character. Like the early Worcester examples, the patterns were principally confined to blue flowers, etc., on a white ground. In this style and color, the Caughley works were superior, in many respects, to their competitors.

Turner set about enlarging the factory. He completed his improvements in 1775, and in 1780, he visited France, to investigate the methods employed in the porcelain factories at Paris.

He brought back several skilled workmen, who aided him in his subsequent innovations. On his return from France, he developed an early or predecessor form of the 'willow pattern'. About the same time, he produced the 'Brosely blue dragon pattern'.

Turner made porcelain willow pattern tea services with richly gilt edges, also fluted cups and saucers marked S and the letter B in gold to denote Brosely (where churchwarden pipes were made).

Turner's exploitation of blue-printing techniques brought him success; he issued a wide range of patterns, including sporting subjects, views, and commemorative pieces (such as that showing the world's first all-iron bridge built nearby in 1779) that were embellished with elaborate scrolled or brocaded borders.

In 1798 or 1799, he retired from the business, which passed into the hands of John Rose, a former apprentice, who carried it on together with his own works at Coalport under the name Rose & Co.

Thomas Turner lived at Caughley Place in an elegant French château, which was pulled down after his death.

THOMAS MINTON, DESIGNER

The famous porcelain which bears the name Minton was first made towards the end of the 18th century. Minton engraved the original Willow pattern plate for Turner and was the founder of the historic Minton's. He started his own business at Stoke about 1790.

Thomas Minton was born at Wyle Cop, Shrewsbury, in 1765. He was an apprentice to Thomas Turner at Caughley, near Broseley, in Shropshire, and then worked for Spode in London.

At the age of twenty-three or so, he was established as a master engraver in Staffordshire where he engraved the famous "willow" pattern.

Five years later, he began the manufacture of pottery on a small scale. Not until 1798 is he stated to have seriously begun the production of china ware.

The manufacture of porcelain was continued for ten or twelve years, but not on an exceptionally large scale. After a cessation of about ten years, the making of porcelain was resumed in 1821. The Minton porcelain of the period 1798-1810 is, however, that which is sought for by collectors of old china. On the following page is represented a bowl of this period in the South Kensington Museum.

It is well potted and of excellent body, into which Cornish china clay and china stone entered. Frequently, the decoration exhibits a certain degree of originality of design and refinement of color unusual in the porcelain of the time.

In later times, the successors of Thomas Minton have been distinguished for their recognition of the work of Continental ceramic artists. Carrier de Belleuse worked at Minton's, so did M. L. Solon, whose exquisite low-relief sculptures in *pâté-sur-pâté* [ii](for so they may be called from their manner of production) are unrivalled for delicacy and invention in the domain of ceramic art.

Minton's early mark, which is painted over glaze, was a direct imitation of that of Sèvres. A number often accompanies this mark. A later mark, previous, however, to the impressed name MINTON, is an enameled or gilt ermine spot.

The tale of the willow pattern is well known as being a western fabrication and has no true place in Chinese mythology.

It seems, nevertheless, to express something quintessentially Chinese, which is probably why it captured the popular western imagination at the time. Thomas Minton's pattern, and the story, was later constructed to boost sales of the crockery.[iii]

This was then, the willow pattern designed from the Oriental and engraved for Thomas Turner of Caughley Hall in the county of Salop. It was extensively used in the decoration of the Caughley (Turner) or Salopian wares, each of these names having been applied to this factory whose china is sometimes marked with a "C" or crescent and sometimes with an "S" alone, or accompanied by a cross or crossed swords, all painted roughly in blue under glaze.

Versions of Blue Willow

The popularity of the willow pattern induced other factories to apply to Thomas Minton for his design, and he sold his copperplates widely; but in each one he made some slight alteration, either in the number of trees, or in the fret of the fence, or in the amount of fruit borne by the apple or orange tree, or in the borders.

A careful study of these variations will not only prove of interest to the collector but will materially aid in determining the locale of a doubtful piece. Thus, in Spode's copy of the original Caughley plate, there are five trees, a more elaborate fence, and thirty-two apples.

The essential Chinese pattern has numberless variations in which the willow holds a prominent place. The constant introduction of this tree into Chinese paintings is accounted for by its being an ever-present object in their landscapes.

In gardens, by waterways, all over China, willows abound and grow to an immense size. They are referenced in many ways and for various reasons.

"Because Ki K'ang celebrated not only as a musician and man of letters but as a disciple of Silenus, and also for the knowledge of alchemy, loved to study it under the shade of the willow tree, a Chinese from that time forward held the willow sacred to that pursuit. "

The willow is also accredited with supernatural power, for the Buddhists believed that water sprinkled from its leaves has the effect of purification, and the warding off of evil spirits is another of its many virtues. Therefore, frequently, willow boughs may be seen hanging from the roofs of houses or suspended over the doors. It is said that Wang Chang, a rebel who lived over a thousand years ago, used willow branches to indicate the dwellings of his followers thus ensuring their immunity from molestation; and ever since the willow has been regarded as an omen of peace and safety.

Amongst the willow patterns is one known by the name of "Pagoda", the second period design. In it, the mandarin's house or pagoda, is on the left; the fence, which is shorter than the story pattern, is filled in with a swastika fret; a mystic diagram of great antiquity regarded in China as a symbol of Buddhist heart. There are trees and a wall behind the house, and a bank with two trees on the opposite or right side of the river; a bridge on which stand two men crosses the stream and a butterfly border encircles the plate.

This border is a complicated affair composed of conventional "petals and fish motifs", butterflies, trellis patterns, and the Joo-e or head of the scepter of longevity. Minton engraved the "Pagoda" design for Spode.

Although there are distinct willow patterns and periods of such patterns, they are often so mutilated and curtailed to suit the especial shape or size of the piece to be decorated as to appear practically unrecognizable. Others, again, vary in many of the details.

The doves are absent in one, the bridge in another, the number of figures are not the same, the willow maybe wanting in the foreground, yet flourishing in such magnificent proportions on Chang's distant island as to suggest the use of a telephoto lens in his portraiture.

A curious specimen is sometimes shown on a cup and saucer marked with a square in imitation of the Oriental, but having within the square a crescent, a T, a C, an S, and what are evidently intended for crossed swords, thus combining the numerous designations of the Caughley (Turner) and Salopian ware.

The "pagoda" pattern is also given to the willow pattern in old and modern Davenport, Rockingham, or

Chester, another china, besides a variety of designs on Oriental porcelain.

One pattern on a pear-shaped jar has a lion and two figures saluting one another in an open space, a third stands in a doorway above a flight of steps. There is the pagoda, the fence, and the island, but only a sketchy willow in the far distance.

Similar figures are to be seen on tolitoli jars (jars with lids) but their surroundings are different. Here there is no fence, but a bridge with one figure crossing it. There are boats and three birds at the very top of the picture.

These are fine specimens of blue and white mandarin, and as is customary in this particular china, they all have two large and four small battalions and frames of raised porcelain, between which the groundwork is composed of a series of tiny hemispheric spots known by the Chinese as "chicken's flesh" or "shagreen". These spots, being devoid of glaze, appear dull white on the vitreous enamel. Flowers scattered here and there complete the decoration and the coloring is of rich deep blue. When shagreen is present, the painting is generally of fine quality.

Yet another version of the willow pattern may be found on a stand and at the bottom of the basket with reticulated sides. This open work is supposed to represent bamboo, the joints appearing above and below in rotation. The broadband of deep blue, with an almost invisible diaper pattern running through it, has its heavy effect light and on the inside by the dagger border, a true Nanking design which was copied by Minton for Spode.

In pottery as well as in china, the old willow pattern is continuously before our eyes. It decorates our breakfast, dinner, and tea services. It appears on the kitchen plate, in the homely dresser, as well as adorning the sides of priceless vases and dainty dishes, cups, soup ladles, and specimens of all kinds. The fecundity of this pattern almost passes belief when we consider what is left and what must have gone before.

Blue Willow Tolitoli Jar

BLUE WILLOW LEGEND 1

Familiar ever since the first use of blue in English pottery than any other design put upon tableware. However, despite this fact, a surprising amount of ignorance or half-knowledge concerning it still persists. The Chinese story, which inspired the English potter apprentice, Thomas Minton, to compose and engrave the design to illustrate it may best be given in the form of one of the delightful bits of verse which formerly were taught to children along with their nursery rhymes.

"So, she tells me a legend centuries old
Of a Mandarin rich in lands and gold,
Of Koong-se fair and Chang the good,
Who loved each other as lovers should.
How they hid in the gardener's hut awhile,
Then fled away to the beautiful isle.
Although a cruel father pursued them there,
And would have killed the hopeless pair,
But kindly power, by pity stirred,
Changed each into a beautiful bird.
Here is the orange tree where they talked,
Here they are running away,
And over at the top you see
The birds making love alway."

The large pagoda on the right of the design, as reproduced from an old pattern, is the palace of the wealthy Mandarin, while upon the terrace stands the summerhouse where Koong-se, the lovely daughter of the Mandarin, was kept prisoner that she might be concealed from Chang, her father's secretary, who loved her and whom she wished to marry.

However, as the story runs in old China, Chang was poor, and the Mandarin had selected a wealthy suitor for his daughter's hand. From her chamber in the prison, the unhappy maiden watched the willow tree blossom while yet the peach tree was only in bud. While she moped, she wrote love sonnets and verses in which she voiced the hope that before the peach blossoms appeared, she might be free.

Chang, however. found a means to communicate with Koong-se once by sending a note in a tiny coconut shell, which with the aid of a small sail made its way to the captive maiden. Koong-se replied by scratching on an ivory tower to the challenge, "Do not wise husbandmen gather the fruits they fear will be stolen?" and, putting the tablet in the boat, she sent it back to her lover.

Chang received the message, acted on the gentle hint, hurried across the sea, donned a disguise, entered the Mandarin's garden despite the barricades which had been erected to keep him away, and eloped with Koong-se.

The father gave chase, and there are on the bridge the three may be seen, Chang carrying a box of jewels, Koong-se with the distaff in her hand, and the angry Mandarin with a whip.

The lovers escaped, however, entered the little boat, and sailed away to Chang's house on the island, where they lived happily until the jilted wealthy suitor discovered them and burned their home.

Then, from out of the ashes of Chang and Koong-se who perished in their bamboo grove, their spirits arose Phoenix-like in the form of white doves, the lovers, who forever hover over the scenes of their earthly happiness.

Another story, a nursery version, with an appropriate moral is: the naughty lovers were overtaken by a terrible storm on their way to Chang's island home. The waves, mountains high, beat against and sank their frail bark, and the fond lovers received a watery grave for their disobedience, but their spirits were united in the skies.

Nearly all Staffordshire potters at one time or another used the willow pattern, or a variance of it. Some of the English designs, erroneously called willow, have but two men on the bridge, or one man, or they have no boat or birds, being in reality merely arrangements of Oriental motifs - trees, pagodas, fences, bridges, to suit the fancy of individual potters, the borders, vary with the pattern In the center , the butterfly, Joo-e dagger, fish roe, fret, etc. etc. with their own adaptations, offering a separate subject for speculation and identification. The scope of this book, however, forbids an extensive review of this remarkably interesting study of Oriental influences upon the early ceramic art of Europe.

More than 200 years ago, the Dutch merchants brought from China several remarkable specimens of porcelain. Among the tea sets were sets of a blueish white background, with landscapes and figures in dark blue. A prominent object in the design was a willow tree. And the Chinese willow pattern soon became the favorite.

Many people can remember that, when they were little children, they used to sit at their grandmothers' tables and study the blue cups and saucers and plates, wondering what the patterns meant, or inventing stories of their own to suit them.

Most children no doubt fancy that China was a strange country, where trees and birds, houses, and people were altogether different from our own. A bright lady wrote:

"The color of the country is kind of dirty blue,
With chaotic land and water here and there appearing through
Interspersed with funny bridges and past that seemed to glide
Two very funny houses upon the other side
There are frightful flowers growing upside down and inside out
Trees with caterpillars laden, some with roots and some without."

Blue Willow Legend 2

This strange Chinese picture has a meaning and is not a mere model, as our grandmother may have thought. On the right of the plate is a lordly Mandarin's country house, in the garden by the side of a river. The house is two stories high and has a tea pavilion in front, all of which show the rank and wealth of the Mandarin. In the garden is a tree with mulberries on it and another full of oranges, to show what a fruitful garden it is.

Around the estate is a bamboo fence, and spanning the river is a bridge. Behind the house is a little gardener's cottage, to show how poor and humble the gardener is. In another poor house, on an island in the river, lives the young gardener's mother. On the bridge are the gardener and the Mandarin's daughter, and behind them comes the Mandarin himself with a long whip. Last of all, there is the mournful willow tree, and in the air a pair of turtle doves with joined beaks. The story connecting all these figures is as follows.

Long ago, when the moon was young, there lived an illustrious Mandarin, who had an only daughter, named Koong-se, more beautiful than all the stars of heaven. Her father intended her to marry some great and rich noble like himself and kept her shut up in his country palace in the midst of a beautiful garden walled in with a high bamboo fence. The gardener was a young man named Chang, who was so handsome, with his almond-shaped eyes, his shining skin, and his slender pigtail, that the fair Koong-se, peeping through her bamboo lattice and seeing him at work, straightway fell in love with him.

Thus, one day, when he was training some roses near her window, she looked out and slyly dropped at his feet a choice sweetmeat, in return for which he climbed the lattice and stuck a rose through the slats. That night when he went in to see his mother who lived on an island in the river, he told her of his adventures and bewailed his ill luck because as an humble gardener, he could never hope to marry the lordly Mandarin's beautiful daughter. However, the mother, who was a shrewd woman, told him to pluck up courage for Koong-se might even yet be his wife.

Now his mother reared silkworms on her little island and spun silk for the Mandarin's daughter, the next time that she carried this silk to the Fair Lady, she told her quietly that the gardener worshipped her shadow and kissed the very tracks which her little feet had left in the garden walk.

And so, in time a plan was arranged whereby Koong-se was on a certain night to run away with her lover, being sure to bring with her a box full of her father's golden jewels in order that they might all live together in comfort.

The mother would hide the maiden and the money in her hut on the island, where none would ever dream of looking for them, and the Mandarin should be made to believe that a robber had stolen the money, and that his daughter had drowned herself.

This plan was so far conducted that the lovers succeeded in escaping unseen through the garden and to the bridge, bearing between them, suspended on a stout bamboo pole, a treasure chest full of gold and jewels.

However, it happened that just as they stepped up on the bridge, at the other end of which Chang's mother awaited them, the illustrious Mandarin awakened from his sleep.

He turned his face to the open doorway and saw his only daughter running away with the gardener and his own box of money. Seizing a stout whip, the Mandarin rushed after the couple and overtaking him on the bridge, grasped Chang by his pigtail, twisted it around his throat, beat him until he was senseless, and ended by throwing him off the bridge into the river, where he immediately sank.

When poor Koong-se saw her lover's cruel fate, she at once sprang into the water after him and was drowned with him.

Strange to say, the bodies could never be found, but near the spot where they sank a beautiful willow[iv] sprang up by magic. It stretches drooping arms above the water and sighs night and day a mournful dirge for the departed lovers.

In its branches, after a few days, a couple of turtledoves appeared and built a nest, and there they would bill and coo the livelong day. For the souls of the unfortunate lovers had taken the shape of doves (so the fable tells), and thus found the happiness they had longed for but lost.

Blue Willow Legend 3

Once upon a time, there was a beautiful Princess named Koong-se, in China, the land of the tea plant.

This was in the time of Emperor Hwang, and his chief Mandarin, Tso Ling, a rich old man, the father of the lovelorn Princess named Koong-se.

She and her father lived in a magnificent pagoda, two stories in height, a rare thing in China at the time. The wealth and resources of the owner are indicated by its being of two stories in height, a most extraordinary thing in China, by the existence of outbuildings at the back and by the large and rare trees which are growing up on all sides of the main building.

This house belonged to a Mandarin of great power and influence, who had amassed considerable wealth and served the Emperor in a department corresponding to our Department of Revenue – collecting excise taxes. The work, as is the case in other places besides China, was performed by an active secretary, named Chang, for the business of the master consisted in receiving kickbacks and bribes from the merchants, at whom smuggling and illegal traffic he winked, in exact proportion, to the illegal fees he was paid for it.[v]

The wife of the Mandarin had, however, died suddenly. The Mandarin requested the Emperor to allow him to retire from his arduous duties. He was particularly urgent in his suit because the merchants had begun to talk loudly of the unfairness and dishonesty of the Mandarin (serving as the Chinese manager of the customs fees).

The death of his wife was a fortunate excuse for the old Mandarin, and in accordance with his petition, an order signed by the vermilion pencil[vi] of his Imperial Majesty, the Emperor was issued to another merchant who had paid a handsome douceur[vii] to his predecessor.

The Mandarin retired to the luxurious estate, as illustrated on the plate, taking with him his only daughter, Koong-se, and his accountant secretary Chang. He had retained Chang's services for a few months to put his accounts in such a state as to bear scrutiny, if, from any unforeseen circumstances, he should be called to produce them. When the faithful Chang had completed this duty, he was discharged.

Too late however! The youth had seen and fallen in love with the Mandarin's daughter.

Koong-se was an exceptionally beautiful girl, and since her father was a rich man, she always dressed in the softest, brightest silks money could buy.

Her favorite dresses were of peach-colored silk, embroidered with silver. If you could have seen her sitting on her balcony, on a moonlit night, with flowers entwined in her hair, and the shimmering peach-colored silk falling in soft folds about her feet, you would have thought her worthy of marrying a Prince.

However, Koong-se did not want to marry a Prince. She had fallen in love with Chang, her father's accountant secretary, who lived in the island cottage you will find at the top of the plate.

Chang was only a commoner, and Koong-se was the daughter of a nobleman. Still, their love grew, and they met beneath a willow tree in the garden.

At sunset, Koong-se was observed to linger with her maid on the steps which led to the banquet room, and as the twilight came on, she stole away down the path to a distant part of the grounds; and there the young lovers, on the last evening of Chang's engagement, vowed mutual promises of love and constancy.

On many an evening afterwards, when Chang was supposed to be miles away, lovers' voices in that place might have been heard amongst the orange trees. As darkness came on, the huge peonies which group on the fantastic wall had their gorgeous petals shaken off as Chang scrambled through their crimson blossoms.

With the assistance of the lady's handmaid, these interviews were obtained without the knowledge of the old Mandarin; for the lovers well knew the harsh fashion of the country, and that their stations in life being unequal, the father would never consent to the union. Chang's merit, however, was known, and the affectionate wishes of the young couple pictured a time when such an obstacle would be removed by his success. They believed, as they hoped, that the year of their fancy had only two seasons - springtime and summer.

By some means, at last the knowledge of one of these interviews came to the old man who was enraged about this. He said, "Ye shall not marry this youth who is not of a royal house; my daughter of the Orient must wed a Prince".

From that time, he forbade his daughter to go beyond the walls of the house; the youth was commanded to discontinue his visits upon pain of death, and to prevent his chivalrous courage from any chance of gratification, the Mandarin imprisoned Koong-se. He ordered a tall fence of zig-zag wood to be built across the pathway from the extremity of the wall to the water's edge, encircling the pavilion.

The Mandarin dismissed the lady's handmaid, too, her place supplied by an old domestic, whose heart was as withered as her shriveled face.

To provide for his daughter's imprisonment and to enable her to take fresh air, he also built a suite of apartments adjoining his banquet room and jutting out over the water's edge up on terraces, upon which the young lady might walk in security. These apartments had no exit but through no exit but through the banquet hall, in which the Mandarin spent the greatest part of his time.

Being completely surrounded by water, the father rested content that he should have no further trouble from clandestine meetings. As also the windows of his sitting room looked out upon the waters, any attempt at communication by means of a boat would be at once seen and frustrated by him.

Completing the disappointment of the lovers, he went still further. He betrothed his daughter to a wealthy friend, a Ta-jin, or Duke of high degree, whom she had never seen. The Ta-jin was her equal in wealth and in every respect but age, which greatly preponderated on the gentleman's side.

Koong-se had never seen the Ta-jin, but her father came to her one evening, as she was sitting on her balcony, which overhung the river and told her he had made arrangements for her marriage.

"Oh, no! no!", sobbed Koong-se. "I love Chang! I cannot marry anyone else."

"Chang shall never be your husband," replied the Mandarin sternly. "I have promised the Ta-jin that you shall be married to him when the peach tree blossoms."

The nuptials were, as usual, determined upon without any consultation of the lady; and the wedding was to occur "at the fortunate age of the moon, when the peach tree should blossom in the spring." The willow tree was in blossom when the peach tree had scarcely formed its buds. Poor Koong-se shuddered at what she called her doom and feared and trembled as she watched the buds of the peach tree, whose branches grew close to the walls of her prison.

But her heart was cheered by a happy omen; a bird came and built its nest in the corner above her window.

The willow tree was in blossom then, for it was quite early in the year.

The peach would not bloom until the spring ; but every day after this Koong-se watched the buds of the peach tree, which grew close to her window, unfolding, and she watched them with dread and sorrow in her heart. "Is Chang dead? Or has he forgotten all about me ?" She wondered to herself.

However, Chang was not dead, neither had he forgotten; he thought of her night and day, and at last one evening he sent her a message.

One day, when she had sat on the narrow terrace for several hours, watching the little architect carrying straws and feathers to its future home, the shades of evening came upon her, and her thoughts reverting to interviews that were associated with the hour, she did not retire as usual, but disconsolately gazed upon the waters. Her abstraction was disturbed by half a coconut shell, which was fitted with a miniature sail and which floated gently close to her feet.

With the aid of her parasol, she reached the miniscule boat from the water. Her delighted surprise at its contents caused her to exclaim aloud in such a manner as to bring the old servant to her side, and nearly to lead to a discovery; but Koong-se was ready with a plausible excuse and dismissed the woman.

As soon as she was gone, she anxiously examined the little boat. In it she found a bead she had given to her lover - sufficient evidence from whose hands the little boat had come; Chang had launched it on the other side of the water. there was also a piece of bamboo paper, and in light characters were written some Chinese verses.[viii]

"The nest yon winged artist builds,
Some robber bird[ix] shall tear away.

46

So, yields her hopes the affianced bride,
The wealthy lord's reluctant prey."
"When the willow fades away ,
And the peach tree groweth gay
Tell me, sweetheart, can it be
They will steal my love from me ?"

"He must have been near me," she murmured, "for he must have seen my bird's nest by the peach tree." She read :
"The fluttering bird prepared a home,
In which the spoiler soon shall dwell.
Forth goes the weeping bride, constrain'd:
A hundred ears, the triumph swell.
"Mourn for the tiny architect,
A stronger bird hath ta'en its nest.
Mourn for the hapless stolen bride,
How vain the hope to sooth her breast!"

Koong-se burst into tears, but hearing her father approaching, she hid the little boat in the folds of her loose flowing robe. When he was gone, she read the verses repeatedly and wept over them.

Upon further examination, she found upon the back these words, in the peculiar metaphorical style of Oriental poetry – "as this boat sails to you, so all my thoughts tend to the same center; but when the willow blossom droops from the bough, and the peach tree unfolds its buds, your faithful Chang will sink with the Lotus blossoms beneath the deep waters.[x]

There will he see the circles on the smooth river, when the willow blossom falls upon it from the bough - broken away like his love from its parent stem." As a sort of postscript was added, "Cast your thoughts upon the waters as I have done, and I shall hear your words."

Koong-se well understood such metaphorical language, and trembled as she thought of Chang's threat of self-destruction.[xi] Having no other writing materials, she sought her ivory tablets, and with the needle she had been using for embroidery, she scratched her answer in the same strain in which her lover had addressed her. This was her reply:

"Do not wise husband men gather their fruits they fear will be stolen?

The sunshine lengthens

And the vineyard is threatened to be spoiled by the hands of strangers.

The fruit you most prize will be gathered,

When the willow blossom groups upon the bough.

When the peach tree blooms, sweetheart,

Thou and I must weep and part .

Hasten then take the prize

Ere 'tis seen by robber's eyes."

She knew that her lover would understand this flowery language, and with much doubting, she placed her tablets in the little boat, and after the manner of her countrywomen, she placed within a stick of frankincense. When it became dark, she lighted the frankincense and launched the little boat upon the stream. And leaning over the balcony, she watched it sail away into the darkness of the night.

The current gradually drew it away, and it floated safely until she could trace it no longer in the distance. That no accident should have overturned the boat or extinguish the light, she had been taught to believe was a promise of good fortune and success, so with a lighter heart she closed her casements and retired to rest.

"He will come for me before my wedding day", she said softly to herself.

The night air was full of the scent of flowers, and everything was still. Koong-se half-imagined she could hear the blossoms on the willow tree sighing faintly and saying, "It will be too late - we are dying!"

For Chang had promised the last time they met, that he would come for her while the willow was still in blossom.

And she thought she heard the buds on the peach tree replying, "We are nearly ready to open. Then she will marry the Ta-jin!"

Chang, on the farther bank of the river, waited to draw his frail little bark to land, and when he read the verse on the ivory tablets, his smile went up to the corners of his eyes, as Chinese smiles generally do; and he walked into the gardener's cottage where he was stopping, and called the gardener and his wife.

"Do you know when the Ta-jin is coming?"

"The betrothal feast is fixed for next Thursday, for the moon will then be lucky", replied the old man.

"The Mandarin has ordered his gardeners to take six dozen carp out of the fish ponds, and there are to be golden and silver pheasants on the table, and boar's head and roast peacock. "

"And six barrels of wine to be bestowed," continued his wife. "And as many oysters as his guests can eat."

"The servants say that that the Ta-jin is bringing his bride such a treasure chest of jewels as never was seen," said the gardener. "A necklace of pearls - each pearl as big as a sparrow's egg – "

"Pigeons egg, stupid!" interrupted the wife.

"Sparrows egg, imbecile!" he retorted.

"It doesn't matter which," Chang broke in. "What I want to know is whether you could lend me one of the servants dresses and smuggle me into the banqueting room that night!"

"It is impossible," replied the gardener, shaking his head.

The old couple knew all about Chang's love story, but they were afraid of helping him. Neither of them dared to risk the displeasure of such a rich and powerful Mandarin as Koong-se's father.

Days and weeks passed on, but no more little boats appeared; all communication seemed to have been cut off, and Koong-se began to doubt the truth of the infallible omen. The blossom upon the willow tree - for she watched it many an hour - seemed about to wither, when a circumstance occurred which gave her additional grounds for this distrust.

The old Mandarin entered his daughter's apartment one morning in high good humor. In his hands he bore the large treasure chest full of rare jewels, which he showed her and said they were to be gifts from the Ta-jin, or Duke, to whom he had betrothed her. He congratulated her upon her good fortune and left her saying, "that the wealthy man was coming that day to perform some of the preliminaries of the wedding, by taking food and wine in her father's house."

Koong-se's hopes all vanished and she found her only relief in tears. Like the netted bird, she saw the snare drawing closer and closer, but possessed no power to escape the toils.

The Duke came, his servants beating gongs before him, and shouting out his achievements in war. The number of his titles was great, and the lanterns on which they were inscribed, were magnificent. Owing to his rank, he was borne in a sedan, to which were attached eight porters, showing his rank to be that of a viceroy.

The old Mandarin gave him a suitable reception and dismissed his followers. The gentlemen then sat down to the introduction feast according to custom, and many were the "cups of salutation" which were drunk between them, until at last they became boisterous in their merriment. The next few days passed in preparation for the betrothal feast.

Servants were running here and there all the time; the Mandarin never stopped giving orders from morning until night; the banqueting hall was swept and strewn with sweet-scented leaves and the walls and roof hung with colored silk lanterns and fans .

Everyone was happy and busy except Koong-se, who sat on her balcony, with her embroidery lying idle on her lap, and her eyes gazing wistfully across the river which separated her from her lover.

On the morning of the betrothal feast, the peach tree was covered with lovely pink blossoms, while the willow blossoms hung faded and drooping on the tree.

This made Koong-se so sad, she could not stay on the balcony; she went into her room and sat on the couch, with her head resting on her hands, watching her attendants as they spread out on the floor the luxurious silk dresses that the Ta-jin had sent as gifts to his bride.

They were all the colors of the rainbow, pale blue, and pink, and yellow, and purple, embroidered in gold and silver, and one of them was peach-colored silk, embroidered with pearls.

"This is just the dress for the bride," said the woman. But Koong-se shook her head. "I will not wear peach color anymore," she said.

At noon, the Ta-jin sent his servant with the treasure chest of jewels of which the gardener and his wife had spoken, and the Mandarin had shown her.

There were diamonds and rubies in it of such size that the Emperor himself would not have despised them. And the necklace of pearls went twice around Koong-se's neck, and nearly to her waist.

At last, her attendants persuaded her to allow them to dress her for her betrothal and they chose a beautiful blue silk dress, embroidered all over with golden butterflies, because in China  butterflies are looked upon as a symbol of married happiness. And they fastened the pearls around her throat and put some shining jewels in her hair.

"For she is going to be a great lady - the wife of a Duke," they said. "Flowers in the hair are only for common people."

"Now leave me quite alone," commanded Koong-se when they had finished.

She was tired of all their foolish talk about the Ta-jin and wanted to step out once more and see if the willow blossoms were quite faded, and if there was no message from Chang sailing to her across the water.

The noise of revelry and the shoutings of the Mandarin and Duke seemed to have attracted a stranger to the house, who sought alms at the door of the banquet room. The woman went away but came back in a moment to tell her that one of the servants wished to speak to her.

His tale being unnoticed, he took from the porch an outer garment which had been left there by one of the servants, and thus disguised, he spread the screen across the lower part of the banquet hall; passing forwards, he came to Koong-se's apartment.

"Let him come in," said Koong-se impatiently. The young man who entered wore a long blue cotton robe and a broad straw hat which had concealed his face, but as soon as they were alone he took off the hat, making her a low sweeping bow, and Koong-se saw that it was Chang himself. For a moment she could not believe it, but when he took her in his arms, and kissed her, crumpling up all the golden butterflies in his eagerness, she knew it was really her lover, who had come to save her from marrying the Ta-jin.

"How did you get here ?" she asked, sobbing with joy.

"I disguised myself as a beggar," said Chang, showing her the rags he wore under his blue robe. "But when I came to the banqueting room, to ask for alms, everyone was too busy to listen to me. Thus, I managed to slip behind the screen they had spread across the lower end of it and find my way out to your room. "

"And this?" said Koong-se, touching his servant's dress.

"One of the servants happened to have left it behind the screen. And now, Koong-se, how can I disguise you?

For we must pass behind the screen again, and through the banqueting room door into the garden, and across the bridge to the gardener's cottage."

It was Chang who had crossed the banquet room. He besought Koong-se to flee with him "for," said he, "the willow blossom already droops upon the bough".

He glanced quickly around the room and found a garment belonging to Koong-se's old nurse, which covered all her bridal finery, except her pretty little gold-embroidered shoes.

"Never mind my shoes," she said, "I shall run so fast no one will see them."

She took her staff in her hand, because she did not want to be an idle, useless wife to Chang, and she gave him the chest of jewels that the Duke had given her that day to carry.

Although the Ta-jin had given the jewels to Koong-se; perhaps Chang did not know what was in the box, and he was in too great a hurry to ask.

"The willow blossoms droop on the bow, my darling! We must delay no longer," he said.

And indeed, as the lovers crept behind the screen, a light breeze shook the last blossoms of the willow to the ground.

"If my father should see us!" whispered Koong-se, holding her lover's hand very tightly.

"Don't be afraid," said Chang. "I have prayed to the good Genii[xii] not to let him catch us. If he comes near, they will change us into two stars, shining together: or perhaps, two turtle doves. You would not mind that would you?"

"I do not mind anything, except parting from you", replied Koong-se.

Finding that the elders were growing sleepy over their cups, and that the servants were taking the opportunity to get intoxicated elsewhere, Koong-si and Chang stole behind the screen, passed the door, descended the steps, and gained the foot of the bridge, beside the willow tree.

They reached the garden in safety, and Chang led his sweetheart toward the bridge.

But Koong-se's pretty little shoes would not allow her to run very fast after all. Not until then did the old Mandarin become aware of what was going on - but he caught a glimpse of his daughter in the garden, and raising an outcry, staggered out after them himself. When they got to the foot of the bridge, the Mandarin came rushing down the garden path with a whip in his hand.

"Stop! Stop!" he cried furiously. "Will no one stop the thief who has stolen my daughter?"

Chang put Koong-se in front of him, and she ran across the bridge first with her distaff[xiii], while he followed her with the chest of jewels. Behind them came the Mandarin, brandishing his whip.

To represent this part of the story are the three figures upon the bridge. The first is the lady Koong-se, carrying her embroidery distaff and the emblem of virginity; the second is Chang, the lover, carting away the coffer of jewels; and the third is the old Mandarin, the lady's father, whose paternal authority and rage are supposed to be indicated by the whip which he bears in his hand.

The Chinese artist could not place the old gentleman in perspective - to be seen in any other situation that in the unnatural proximity in which we find him. The sketch simply indicates the flight and the pursuit and is graphic enough for the purpose.

The old Mandarin, tipsy as he was, had some difficulty in keeping up the pursuit, and Chang and Koong-se eluded him without much effort.

The Ta-jin fell into an impotent rage on hearing what had occurred, and so great was his fury that he frosted at the mouth and was practically smothered in his drunken passion. Those few of his servants, indeed, who were sober enough to have successfully pursued the fugitives, or detained to attend upon the Duke, who was supposed to be in a fit, until the lovers had made good their escape.

During the following days, every suggested plan was adopted to discover to what place the undutiful daughter had fled. When the servants returned evening after evening and brought no intelligence providing any hope of detecting her place of seclusion, the old Mandarin gave himself up to despair and became prey to low spirits and ill humor.

The Duke, however, was more active and persevering, and employed spies at every village for miles around. He made a solemn vow of vengeance against Chang, and congratulated himself that, by his power as magistrate of the district, when Chang should be discovered, he would exercise his plenary authority and put Chang to death for the theft of the jewels.

The lady, too, he said should die[xiv] unless she fulfilled the wishes of her parent, not for his own gratification, but for the sake of public justice.

In the meantime, the lovers had retreated to an humble dwelling at no great distance from the Mandarin's establishment. They had found safety in the concealment afforded to them by the handmaid of Koong-se, who had been discharged as a consequence of affording Chang an opportunity of clandestinely meeting his love in the gardens of her former home.

The husband of this handmaid, who worked for the Mandarin as a gardener, and Chang's sister, were witnesses of the betrothals and the simple marriage of the fugitives.

They passed their time in closed concealment. They never appeared abroad except after nightfall, when they wandered across the rice paddies or in terraced gardens on the mountainsides, breathing the rich perfume of star jasmine, or the more delicate scent of the flowers of the orange or the citron groves.

From the gardener they learned the steps taken by their pursuers and were prepared to elude them for a considerable time.

But at last, the Mandarin having issued a proclamation, that if his daughter would forsake Chang and return to her old home, he would forgive her, the young man expressed himself so exceedingly joyful at the sign of his Master's relenting, that suspicion was attached to him. The poor house in which they resided was ordered to be watched.

The reader will find this house significantly represented at the foot of the bridge. It is only one story in height and of the simplest style of architecture. The ground about it is cultivated; the tree that grows nearby is of an unproductive species, being a common fir. The whole place has a sad air of poverty and dullness, which becomes more striking when the richly ornate and sheltered mansion on the other side of the bridge is compared with it.

It had been agreed that, in case any suspicion fell upon the house, the young gardener should not return at the usual hour. Chang and his wife suspected that all was not right when he did not enter at the customary time in the evening. The gardener's wife also saw strange people loitering about and in great sorrow communicated her fears to the newly married pair.

Later in the evening, a soldier entered the house, and after having read the proclamation of the Mandarin, he pointed out the significant advantages which would arise to all parties who assisted in restoring Koong-se and bringing Chang to justice. He told her, moreover, that the house was guarded at the front and reminded her that there could be no escape, as the river surrounded it in every other direction.

The attachment of the gardener's wife to her old mistress was, however, sufficient to enable her to retain her presence of mind. After appearing exceedingly curious as to what rewards she would obtain if she were successful in discovering Chang, she led him to suppose that he was not there, but in a friend's house, to which she would show him if he would first obtain a distinct promise of a reward for her in the handwriting of the Mandarin and the Duke.

The soldier promised to obtain the writing, but told her, to her great disappointment, that he must leave the guard about the house. She dared not object to this, or she felt she would be convicted. Still, she talked as loudly as possible of the impropriety of rough soldiers being left without their commanding officer and thus gave the trembling lovers the opportunity of overhearing what was passing, and of learning the dreadful extremity in which they were placed.

As soon as the officer had gone, a brief conference was held between the lovers and their protector. A few minutes later - an hour at most - was all they could call their own. A score of plans was suggested, examined, cast aside.

There were the suspicious guards, who were ordered to let no person, under any circumstances, pass in the front; and behind was the broad, rapid river. Escape seemed impossible, and, for Chang at least, detection and arrest were death. To attempt to fight through the guard was madness and a man unarmed - and what will become of Koong-se? What was to be done?

It was almost impossible to swim the roaring river when it was most quiet: now it was swollen with the early rains; but the river was the only chance.

"But you will be seen, and be butchered in the water, before you climb the other bank," suggested the gardener's wife.

"It is my only chance," said Chang. thoughtfully, as he stripped off the poupua.[xv]

Koong-se clung to him, but his resolution was firm, and bidding her be of good cheer - that he would get across, and come again to her, he jumped from the window into the stream below, with Koong-se's promise of eternal constancy ringing in his ears.

The struggle was frightful and long before Chang had reached the middle of the torrent, Koong-se's eyelids quivered and closed - she fainted and saw no more. Her faithful attendant laid her upon a rude couch, and seeing the color returning to her lips, gazed out of the window upon the river.

Nothing of Chang was to be seen. The river - the rapid torrent had carried him away – where?

Time passed with every moment seeming an age, and darkness began to come down upon the earth. The poor gardener's wife hung over her pallid mistress and dreaded her questions when consciousness would be restored. The officer had been absent sufficiently long to visit the Duke and Mandarin. Hark! He was even now knocking at the door.

The soldier knocked again before the gardener's wife could bring herself to leave Koong-se, but no other course was left to her. Scarcely knowing why, she securely closed the door of the apartment behind her and drew the screen across to conceal it.

The soldier rudely questioned her as to her delay in opening the door and showed her the document which he had obtained, in which large sums of money and the Emperor's favor were promised to any person who would give up Chang, and restore Koong-se to her father.

She pretended that she could not read the writing and having given the soldier some wine made from rice, she managed to pass a very considerable time in irrelevant matters.

When the officer became impatient, she told him that she thought it would be useless to attempt to catch Chang until it was quite dark, when he would be walking in a neighboring rice field.

Two hours went by, when the officer was called out by one of the men under him, who told him that a messenger had arrived from the Ta-jin, inquiring why the villain Chang had not been brought before him, and requiring an answer from the commanding officer himself.

This gave the gardener's wife time to see what had become of Koong-se. She had fancied she heard some noise in the apartment. With intense curiosity, she pushed the screen aside, opened the door, and peeped into the room. Koong-se was not there.

There were marks of wet feet and dripping garments on the floor and upon the narrow ledge of the window to which she rushed.

A boat had just that instant been pushed off from the shore into the river, and in it, there was no doubt were her mistress and her husband, the brave Chang. The darkness concealed them from the eyes of friends or enemies as the rushing river carried them rapidly away.

The gardener's wife gently closed the window and hastily removed all traces of what had happened. She then cheerfully returned to another part of the house and waited for the officer.

He came, stimulated by a reproof for his delay, and commanded his soldiers to search the house, which they did most willingly, as, upon such occasions, they were accustomed to possessing themselves of everything which could be considered valuable.

Their search was in vain, however, where they neither found traces of the fugitives or anything worth stealing. The jewels were with Chang upon the river, and the gardener was but a poor man.

They suspected that the woman had played a trick on them, but she looked quite oblivious. In a very innocent manner, she persuaded the officer that he had been imposed upon, and that she was sorry she had given him so much trouble.

The boat, with its precious cargo, floated down the river all that night requiring no exertion from Chang, who sat silently watching at the prow, while his young wife slept in the cabin. When the gray of the early morning peeped over the distant mountains, Chang still sat there, and the boat was still rapidly buoyed onwards by the current.

Soon after daylight, they entered the main river, the Yangtze River, and their passage then became more dangerous, requiring considerable management and exertion from the boatman.

Before the sun was well up, they had joined a crowd of boats, and ceased to be singular, sure they were in company with persons who lived wholly upon the river, but who had been engaged in taking westward the usual tribute of salt and rice to his Imperial Majesty's Treasury. To one of the boatmen, he sold a jewel and from another he purchased food with the coin.

Thus, they floated onwards for several days towards the sea, but having at length approached a place where the Mandarins were accustomed to examining all boats outward bound, Chang moored his floating home beside an island in the broad river.

It was but a small piece of ground covered with reeds - but here the young pair resolved to settle down, and to spend the rest of their days in peace. The jewels were sold in the neighboring towns in such a manner as not to excite suspicion, and with the funds thus procured, the persevering Chang was able to obtain all that was necessary, and to purchase a free night to the little island.

It is related of Koong-se, that with her own hand she assisted in building the house, while her husband was applying himself to agricultural pursuits and brought the island into a high state of cultivation.

On referring again to the plate, the reader will find the history of the island significantly recorded by the simple artist. The ground is broken up into lumps, indicating recent cultivation, and the trees around it are smaller in size, indicating their youth.

The diligence of Chang is sufficiently evidenced by how every scrap of ground which could be added to the island is reclaimed from the water. To illustrate this, narrow reefs of land are seen jutting out into the stream.

The remainder of the story is soon told. Chang, having achieved a competence by his cultivation of the land, returned to his literary pursuits and authored an agricultural book. It gained him a great reputation in the province where he resided.

The book was the means of securing the patronage of the wealthy literary men of the neighborhood for his children. One son became a great sage after the death of his father and mother, which occurred in the manner now to be related.

The reputation of Chang's book, although it gained him friends and influence, revealed his whereabouts to his greatest enemy, the Ta-jin, or Duke, whose passion for revenge was unabated. Nor did the Duke long delay the accomplishment of his object. Having waited upon the military mandarin of the river station, and having sworn, by cutting a live cock's head off, that Chang was the person who had stolen his jewels, he obtained an escort of soldiers to arrest Chang.

With his military escort, the Ta-jin attacked the island, having given secret instructions to seize Koong-se and to kill Chang without mercy.

The peaceful inhabitants of the island were wholly unprepared. However, Chang, having refused the party admittance, was run through the body and mortally wounded.

His servants, who were much attached to him, fought bravely to defend their master, but when they saw him fall, they threw down their weapons and fled. Koong-se, in despair, rushed to her apartments, which she set on fire, and perished in flames.

The gods - so runs the tale - cursed the Duke for his cruelty with a foul disease, with which he went down to his grave[xvi] unfriended and unpitied. No children scattered scented paper over his grave.

In benevolence to Koong-se and her lover, they were transformed into two immortal doves, emblems of constancy, which had rendered them beautiful in life and in death undivided.

The next time you come across a willow pattern plate, you must look for them, hovering in the air above the bridge.

On the bridge itself you will see three figures, Koong-se with her distaff, Chang with the jewels, and the Mandarin with his whip.

At one end is the famous willow tree which shed its blossoms on the day of elopement. At the other is the gardener's cottage. At the top of the plate and island, there is another cottage on it, in which Chang had hoped to live with Koong-se.

But instead of that, they built a cozy nest in the garden, from which they could watch the willow and the peach trees bloom and fade without any fear of being parted from each other.

Perhaps the pattern will never be entirely done away with as many love the design who looked at it as merely a pretty blue and white pattern on grandmother's bountiful table, but knowledge of the little China Princess and her lover who make the picture into a story may add another charm to willow-ware. Where, in your mind, as it is in mine, "all the world loves a lover."

BLUE WILLOW POEMS

Old Staffordshire and Shropshire poems of the pattern conclude with these verses:

"In the oft quoted plate two birds are perceived,
High in the heaven above:
These are the spirits of Chang and Koong-se,
A twin pair forever in love."

"Two birds flying high,
A Chinese vessel, sailing by.
A bridge with three men, sometimes four,
A willow tree, hanging o'er.
A Chinese temple, there it stands,
Built upon the river sands.
An apple tree, with apples on,
A crooked fence to end my song."

Another old poem from the late nineteenth-century Shropshire is:

"Two swallows flying high,
A little boat passing by,
A little bridge, with willows over,
Three men going to Dover,
Now Dover church stands very bare,
Twice a week they worship there,
A little tree with apples on,
And plaited palings in the sun."

[i] **Pâte-sur-pâte** is a French term meaning "paste on paste".

[ii] **"Understand Chinese Mythology"** – Teresa Moorey, Author

[iii] **The Willow Tree** The tree represents being structured around the world tree, which has its roots in the lower world, its trunk in the middle world, and its branches in the upper world, these three worlds constitute the home of different sorts of spirits and offer different experiences to the ascending shaman.

The Willow is especially important to the Chinese, being associated with the goddess of compassion, **Kuan Yin**. Kuan means earth, and Yin as we know relates to the force of the feminine. She sprinkles the waters of life with a Willow branch and is often shown riding a dolphin. She is sometimes featured in the myth of Monkey King, helping the pilgrims with her special magic. In Europe, the Willow is associated with death and with unrequited love. It is thought to be weeping, because of the trailing strands formed by its leaves.

[iv] **Customs Fees** are a cost that a country or control agent charges to manage the flow of goods in and out of the country. All products go through Customs before going to the buyer, and there is a fee associated to manage this process.

[v] The **Vermilion Pencil** was the official register of imperial decrees in Imperial China. Like other oriental monarchies, official sanction of all public acts were conveyed by the impression of a seal. Any remark or directive of the emperor of China was written in red, commonly styled "the vermilion pencil."

[vi] The word derives from the Latin adjective *dulcis* meaning "sweet." A **douceur** is a gift or payment - sometimes, but not necessarily, considered a bribe - provided by someone to enhance or "sweeten" a deal.

vii Translated by Sir William Jones, in the Asiatic Transactions

viii **Robber bird**: Cuckoos are common in China.

ix The blossoms of the **water lily** appear to sink after their beauty is past.

x Historically, **suicide** was estimated a virtue rather than a crime in the codes of morals of the Chinese.

xi **Genii**: A guardian of people and places in Roman religion. It first appeared in 18th-century translations of the Thousand and One Nights from the French, where it had been used owing to its rough similarity in sound and sense and further applies to benevolent intermediary spirits, in contrast to the malevolent spirits called demon and heavenly angels, in literature.

xii A **distaff** is a tool used in spinning. It is designed to hold the unspun fibers, keeping them untangled and thus easing the spinning process. It is most commonly used to hold flax, and sometimes wool, but can be used for any type of fiber. Koong-see used her distaff for embroidery thread.

xiii **Disobedience** to parents was **a capital offense** in China parents have power to put their children to death summarily; disobedience is, however, no less common.

xiv **Poupua:** A loose outer garment commonly worn by the higher classes, or by those who seek for literary honors.

xv Historically, it is a great reproach to be childless in China.

Twice a year, relatives sprinkle or burn scented paper upon the graves of their friends or ancestors.

RECOMMENDED READING

Other Books by Jennifer C. Petersen

Available on Amazon in print and Kindle:

http://www.amazon.com/Jennifer-C.-Petersen

17-76 Tea Party Award Winning Recipes

17 Jam and Scone Recipes; 76 Scone Recipes

Lavender Cookbook: Essential Lavender Recipes

Lavender Cookbook: Simple & Delicious Recipes

A Colonial Tea – an historical one-act play

Scone Recipes: Amazing Scone Baking Race – Delicious, Prize-winning Scone Recipes

Thank Goodness! It's Pie Day

History of Tea – It's History and Mystery

Poetic History of Blue Willow

Blue Willow – A Dish of Gossip on a Blue Willow Plate

Blue Willow Plate – The Love Story

Tea Sommelier Journals

Foundations of Tea

Scan Me

www.ingramcontent.com/pod-product-compliance
Lightning Source LLC
Chambersburg PA
CBHW080726280626
47162CB00020B/3088